I0814874

MAY DAY MERRYMAKING & MUNCHIES

Anna Anderhagen

Consulting Editor, Diane Craig, MA/Reading Specialist

Super Sandcastle

An Imprint of Abdo Publishing
abdobooks.com

abdobooks.com

Published by Abdo Publishing, a division of ABDO, PO Box 398166, Minneapolis, Minnesota 55439.

Printed in the United States of America, North Mankato, Minnesota
102024
012025

Design: Layne Halvorsen, Mighty Media, Inc.
Production: Mighty Media, Inc.
Editor: Liz Salzmann
Cover Photographs: Mighty Media, Inc. (recipe photos); Shutterstock Images
Interior Photographs: Adobe Stock, pp. 8 (chocolate chips), 12 (hands), 13 (containers, washing plate), 30 (robin); Mighty Media, Inc. (recipe photos), pp. 10, 14, 15, 16, 17, 18, 19, 20, 21, 22, 23, 24, 25, 26, 27, 29; Shutterstock Images, 1 (rolling pin), 4 (goat), 5 (all), 6 (all), 7 (child), 8 (sprinkles, jelly beans, pudding), 8–9 (licorice, Pocky sticks, food coloring), 9 (all), 10 (bread), 11 (all), 14 (flowers), 16 (flowers), 20 (butterflies), 22 (bouquet), 24 (pizza slice), 28–29 (child), 29 (plate, rolling pin), 30 (shark, flag), 31 (child)
Design Elements: Shutterstock Images (abstract doodles, kitchen utensil doodles)

Library of Congress Control Number: 2024938382

Publisher's Cataloging-in-Publication Data
Names: Anderhagen, Anna, author.
Title: May day merrymaking & munchies / by Anna Anderhagen
Description: Minneapolis, Minnesota : ABDO Publishing, 2025 | Series: Holiday jokes & sweet treats | Includes online resources and index.
Identifiers: ISBN 9781098295202 (lib. bdg.) | ISBN 9798384915256 (ebook)
Subjects: LCSH: Jokes--Juvenile literature. | May Day (Labor holiday)--Juvenile literature. | Holidays--Juvenile literature. | Snack foods--Juvenile literature. | Cooking--Juvenile literature.
Classification: DDC 398.7--dc23

TO ADULT HELPERS

The sweet treats in this series are fun and simple. There are just a few things to remember to keep kids safe. Creating some treats requires the use of hot objects. Also, kids may be using messy materials, such as food coloring. Make sure they protect their clothes and work surfaces. Review the projects before starting and be ready to assist when necessary.

Super Sandcastle™ books are created by a team of professional educators, reading specialists, and content developers around five essential components—phonemic awareness, phonics, vocabulary, text comprehension, and fluency—to assist young readers as they develop reading skills and strategies and increase their general knowledge. All books are written, reviewed, and leveled for guided reading and early reading intervention programs for use in shared, guided, and independent reading and writing activities to support a balanced approach to literacy instruction.

Contents

MAY DAY

Spring is when new plants grow and flowers bloom. It's when animals start having babies. Many ancient **cultures** had spring **festivals** to welcome the warmer weather and **celebrate** these signs of new life.

Ancient Celtic people who lived mainly in Ireland, the United Kingdom, and France held a festival around May 1. It was called Beltane. People lit bonfires, decorated livestock with May flowers, and danced around trees. Later, they danced around **maypoles** instead.

When European **immigrants** arrived in the US, they brought these **traditions** with them. Over time, more ways to **celebrate** May 1st started. In the 1800s, people would leave paper baskets filled with flowers and sweets at neighbors' doors. They would yell "May basket!" and run, hoping not to get caught. Today, May Day is still a popular holiday.

Holiday Hoots!

What kind of flower sleeps on May Day?

A Day-ZZZ.

What do clouds wear during May Day showers?

Thunder-wear.

What did spring say when it was in trouble?

May-Day!

What kind of parties do sheep have on May Day?

Baa-baa-cues!

Which state loves May Day the most?

May-ne.

Did you hear about the gardener who couldn't wait for May Day?

He was so excited, he wet his plants!

What do you call a bee that can't make up its mind on May Day?

A may-bee!

What's a duck's favorite snack on May Day?

Quack-ers!

Sweet Materials

Here are some of the ingredients and tools you will need to make the treats in this book.

Ingredients

- butter
- butterscotch pudding
- candy melts
- candy-coated chocolates
- candy-covered sunflower seeds
- canola oil
- chocolate chips
- chocolate pudding
- cinnamon candies
- colorful candies
- cooking spray
- double-stuffed vanilla sandwich cookies
- food coloring
- graham crackers
- marshmallows
- matcha Pocky sticks
- rainbow sprinkles
- red candy strips
- red licorice ropes
- Rice Krispies cereal
- shredded coconut
- white chocolate chips
- wrapped square taffy candies

Tools

- baking sheet
- bowls
- brightly colored chenille stems
- clothespins
- crinkle-cut paper
- double-sided tape
- googly eyes
- knife or pizza cutter
- lollipop sticks
- measuring cups & spoons
- microwave-safe bowl
- parchment paper
- pony beads
- rolling pin
- round cake pan
- scissors
- sealable plastic bag
- silicone spatula
- skewers
- small cookie cutters
- small pail or vase
- spoons

What did the refrigerator say to the salad?

Lettuce chill!

Marshmallow Tips & Tricks

Some of the recipes in this book include marshmallows. Here are some tips for working with them!

General Tips

- If the marshmallows are stuck together in the bag, pour in a little powdered sugar or **cornstarch**. Shake the bag until the marshmallows separate.
- If the marshmallows are too dry, leave a piece of white bread in the bag overnight. The moisture from the bread will soften the marshmallows.

How do marshmallows communicate with each other?

S'morse code.

How to Cut Marshmallows

- You can use scissors, a pizza cutter, or a knife to cut marshmallows.
- Whatever tool you use, grease it with cooking spray or butter. It will make cutting the marshmallows easier.
- The marshmallows might get squished when you cut them. But they should return to their original shape. If they don't, gently **mold** them back into shape.

When Marshmallows Get Too Sticky

- Sprinkle some powdered sugar on your work surface to keep the marshmallows from sticking to it.
- Grease **utensils** with butter or cooking spray to keep the marshmallows from sticking to them.

Rice Krispie Treat Tip

- Wet your hands when molding Rice Krispie treats into shapes. The water will keep them from sticking to your hands. You can also try dusting your hands with powdered sugar or spraying a little cooking spray on them.

Treats Prep

What is the most polite holiday?

May Day.

Be Safe

- Ask an adult for permission to use kitchen tools and ingredients.
- Ask an adult to help you use the microwave.
- Ask an adult for help when handling sharp or hot objects.
- Clean up spills right away.

Get Ready!

- Wash your hands.
- Clean your work surface before you start.
- Read the list of tools and ingredients for the sweet treat you are making. Set out everything you will need.
- Read the whole recipe at least once before you start.

When You Are Finished

- Let hot treats cool completely.
- Put all the ingredients and tools away.
- Store leftover ingredients to use later.
- Wash all the dishes and cooking tools.
- Clean your work surface.
- Wash your hands before you eat your sweet treats!

Krispie May Day Baskets

Why do marshmallows make good detectives?
They love solving sticky situations!

Ingredients

- 3 tablespoons butter
- 16-ounce package of regular or mini marshmallows
- 6 cups Rice Krispies cereal
- red licorice ropes
- several kinds of candies

Tools

- microwave-safe bowl
- spoon
- measuring cups
- cooking spray
- 3 small bowls
- skewers (optional)

WOW!

1. Put the butter and marshmallows in a microwave-safe bowl. Microwave on high for 2 minutes. Stir the mixture. Microwave for 1 more minute. Stir until smooth.
2. Add the cereal. Stir until the cereal is coated.
3. Grease the small bowls. Put a large spoonful of mixture in each bowl. Press it against the sides of the bowls to form basket shapes.
4. Create handles out of licorice ropes. Press some of the remaining mixture around the ends to hold the handles in place.
5. Place the baskets in the refrigerator for 20 minutes to set.

Tip:

If the handles fall over, prop them up with skewers while the baskets are in the refrigerator. Remove the skewers before adding the candy.

6. Remove the baskets from the refrigerator. Take them out of the bowls.
7. Fill your Krispie May Day Baskets with candies. Give them to friends and neighbors for May Day. Let them know that they can eat the basket too!

Flower Power Garden

Why couldn't the flower ride its bike on May Day?

It lost its petals.

Ingredients

- regular marshmallows
- matcha Pocky sticks
- pastel candy-coated chocolates
- 2 cups premade chocolate pudding
- mini marshmallows
- 2 cups premade butterscotch pudding
- chocolate chips
- 1½ cups shredded coconut
- green and yellow food coloring

SWEET!

Tools

- scissors, pizza cutter, or knife
- cutting board
- large clear bowl
- measuring cups
- large spoon
- sealable plastic bag

1. Cut a marshmallow in half. Poke a Pocky stick into the side of one half of the marshmallow. This is the flower's stem.
2. Stretch out the cut side of the marshmallow a bit. Place one candy in the middle. Add six candies around it. These are the flower petals.
3. Repeat steps 1 and 2 to make more flowers.
4. Spread half the chocolate pudding in the bottom of the bowl. This is the dirt.
5. Add a layer of mini marshmallows. These are the rocks.
6. Spread the butterscotch pudding over the marshmallows. This is the **subsoil**.
7. Add a layer of chocolate chips. These are the pebbles.
8. Spread the rest of the chocolate pudding on top. This is the **topsoil**.

Continued on the next page.

9. Put the shredded coconut in a plastic bag. Add three drops each of green and yellow food coloring. Seal the bag.
10. Shake the bag until the coconut turns light green. Spread it on top of the pudding. This is the grass.
11. Stick the flower stems into the bowl. Break off a bit of some stems to make the flowers different heights.
12. Share your Flower Power Garden with your friends on May Day.

NEAT!
What is the month of May's favorite drink?
Spring water!

Sweet Butterflies

What do you call a butterfly that is passing you?

A flutter-by!

Ingredients

- small candies in different colors
- wrapped square taffy candies

Tools

- brightly colored chenille stems, cut in half
- scissors
- clothespins
- sealable plastic snack bags
- double-sided tape
- googly eyes
- pony beads

1. Clip half of a chenille stem in a clothespin. Twist it behind the clothespin. This is the butterfly's antennae.
2. Fill a plastic bag half full with small candies. Press the air out of the bag and seal it.
3. Pinch the bag in the middle so half the candy is on each side. Twist the bag and clip it with the clothespin. These are the wings.
4. Use double-sided tape to stick three square candies to the clothespin. This is the butterfly's body.

5. Use double-sided tape to stick two googly eyes to the candy closest to the tip of the clothespin. Add a pony bead to the end of each antennae.

6. Repeat steps 1 through 5 to make more butterflies. Give them to your friends and neighbors on May Day!

Cookie Pop Bouquet

What May Day flowers have faces?

Two-lips!

Ingredients

- 12-ounce bag of white candy melts
- blue and yellow food coloring
- double-stuffed vanilla sandwich cookies
- cinnamon candies
- candy-covered sunflower seeds

Tools

- baking sheet
- parchment paper
- microwave-safe bowl
- spoon
- lollipop sticks
- small pail or vase
- crinkle-cut paper

COOL!

1. Line the baking sheet with parchment paper.
2. Put about half the bag of candy melts in a microwave-safe bowl. Microwave for 20 seconds at a time. Stir after each time. Repeat until it is creamy and smooth. Stir in blue food coloring until the candy is the color you want.
3. Working quickly, push a lollipop stick into the side of a cookie. Coat the cookie with melted candy. Place it on the baking sheet.
4. Place a cinnamon candy or sunflower seed in the center of the cookie. Place sunflower seeds around the center candy to make flower petals.
5. Repeat steps 3 and 4 to make more flowers until the bowl is empty.
6. Repeat steps 2 through 5, except use yellow food coloring for the candy melts.
7. Arrange the cookie pops in a pail or vase. Add crinkle-cut paper to hold them up. Invite friends over on May Day to share your Cookie Pop Bouquet!

Why was the florist so happy on May Day?

Because business was blooming!

May Day Candy Pizza

Why was the May Day candy pizza wet?
It got sprinkled on!

YUM!

Ingredients

- red candy strips
- other brightly colored candies
- 13 whole graham crackers
- ⅓ cup butter
- 2 cups white chocolate chips
- 1 teaspoon canola oil
- rainbow sprinkles

Tools

- scissors
- small cookie cutters
- cutting board
- large sealable plastic bag
- rolling pin
- round cake pan
- microwave-safe bowls
- measuring cups & spoons
- spoon
- silicone spatula
- knife or pizza cutter

1. Use scissors and cookie cutters to cut pizza topping shapes out of the candy.
2. Place ten graham crackers in the plastic bag. Press the air out of the bag and seal it. Use a rolling pin to crush the graham crackers into **crumbs**. Put the crumbs in the cake pan.
3. Put the butter in a microwave-safe bowl. Microwave it for 45 seconds or until melted. Pour the melted butter over the graham cracker crumbs. Mix well. Press the mixture down firmly with a spoon. This is the crust.
4. Break three graham crackers apart at the lines. Break each piece in half. This makes 24 small squares. Arrange squares around the edge of the cake pan. This is your crust.
5. Put the white chocolate chips and oil in a microwave-safe bowl. Microwave for 20 seconds at a time. Stir after each time. Repeat until mixture is creamy and smooth

Continued on the next page.

6. Spread the melted chocolate over the crust.
7. Arrange the candy pizza toppings on the pizza. Press them gently into the chocolate. Cover the pizza with sprinkles.
8. Let the pizza cool for about 30 minutes. Cut slices with a knife or pizza cutter. Serve to your friends on May Day!

Knock, knock!

Who's there?

Canoe.

Canoe who?

Canoe pick up some candy pizza for May Day?

WHOA!
Knock, knock!
Who's there?
Eddie.
Eddie who?
Eddie–body home for me to deliver your May Day basket?

Keep Creating!

You've made some **delicious** treats with the recipes in this book! Hopefully you had some laughs with your friends too. But could you make any of the recipes differently? Could you use different ingredients? Or can you think of your own **festive** May Day treat?

Rainbow sprinkles are just one way to decorate a May Day Pizza. You can also use sanding sugar, or another type of sprinkle, such as stars or flowers. Or perhaps you really like chocolate and want to add it to your Krispie May Day Baskets. Use Cocoa Krispies instead of regular Rice Krispies.

Does a treat include an ingredient you don't like? Get creative! Find something else to use that you do like. For example, if you don't like the taste of candy melts, you could add some drops of vanilla extract or other flavoring to it. You could also use pretzel sticks instead of the matcha Pocky sticks for the Flower Power Garden stems.

Why did the cookie go to the doctor?

It felt crumby!

Just use your imagination to keep creating!

Last Laughs

Where did the shark go for spring break?

Finland!

Why are flowers so friendly in spring?

They always have new buds!

What tree is the happiest on May Day?

The May-ple.

Which bird should you never let into a bank?

A robin.

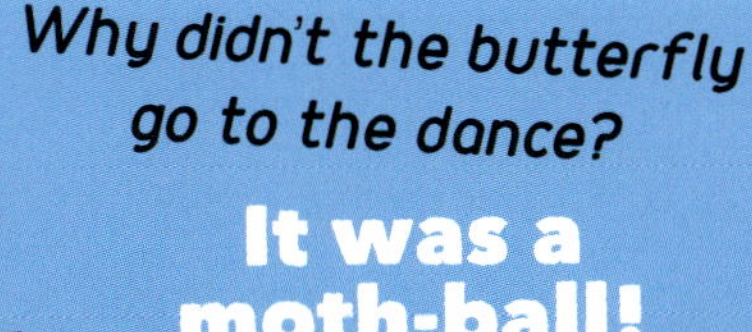

Why didn't the butterfly go to the dance?

It was a moth-ball!

What condiment should you always use on May Day?

Mayo.

How does the sun listen to its favorite music?

On the ray-dio.

What season is it when you're on a trampoline?

Spring-time.

Glossary

celebrate – to observe a holiday with special events.

cornstarch – a powder made from corn that is used in cooking.

crumb – a tiny piece of something, especially food.

culture – the particular behaviors, beliefs, art, and other products of a group of people.

delicious – very pleasing to taste.

festival – a celebration that often happens at the same time each year.

festive – cheerful, bright, and exciting.

immigrant – someone who has left his or her home and settled in a new country.

maypole – a tall pole decorated with ribbons and flowers that people dance around during May Day events.

mold – to work and press into shape with your fingers.

subsoil – a layer of dirt and small rocks under the soil on the surface.

topsoil – the layer of dirt on the surface where grass and plants grow.

tradition – a belief or practice passed through a family or group of people.

utensil – a tool used to prepare or eat food.